Richard Scarry's
Christmas Mice

🐿 A GOLDEN BOOK • NEW YORK

Copyright © 1992 by Richard Scarry. All rights reserved. This 2014 edition was published in the United States by Golden Books, an imprint of Random House Children's Books, a division of Penguin Random House LLC, 1745 Broadway, New York, NY 10019, and in Canada by Random House of Canada, a division of Penguin Random House Ltd., Toronto. Originally published in the United States in a different form as *The Santa Claus Book* by Golden Books in 1965. *The Santa Claus Book* copyright © 1965, renewed 1993 by Penguin Random House LLC. Subsequently published in a different form as *Richard Scarry's Christmas Mice* by Golden Books in 1992. Golden Books, A Golden Book, A Little Golden Book, the G colophon, and the distinctive spine design are registered trademarks of Penguin Random House LLC. A Little Golden Book Classic is a trademark of Penguin Random House LLC.
randomhousekids.com
Educators and librarians, for a variety of teaching tools, visit us at
RHTeachersLibrarians.com
Library of Congress Control Number: 2013941680
ISBN: 978-0-385-38421-6
Printed in the United States of America
15 14 13 12 11 10 9 8

It was early Christmas morning.

Santa had come in the night and left presents for everyone.

No one was awake yet, except for two little mice.

They climbed up the Christmas tree to look at the ornaments.

They looked at the Christmas candies on the shelf.

Then they looked under the tree.

R
IS FOR REINDEER

Santa had put a picture book there . . .

S IS FOR SLEIGH

and a castle with soldiers . . .

and a blue dollhouse . . .

and a bright red racing car.

There were cookies and gingerbread.

There was even a gingerbread house.

Santa had not forgotten
to leave two dolls—one large
and one small . . .

and lots of cuddly toy animals.

There were presents for everyone,
wrapped in pretty papers and ribbons.

And there was a real, live puppy for the whole family.

But had Santa forgotten the two little mice?

No—he had left them a big piece of cheese.

Merry Christmas,
little mice!